How the
Camel
got his Hump

Retold by Robert James

Illustrated by Stefania Colnaghi

PA

Cr ny

www.crabtreebooks.com

Crabtree Publishing Company
www.crabtreebooks.com
1-800-387-7650

PMB 59051, 350 Fifth Ave.
59th Floor,
New York, NY 10118

616 Welland Ave.
St. Catharines, ON
L2M 5V6

Published by Crabtree Publishing in 2012
Printed in Canada 082017/MQ20170616

Series editor: Jackie Hamley
Editor: Kathy Middleton
Proofreader: Reagan Miller
Series advisor: Catherine Glavina
Series designer: Peter Scoulding
Production coordinator and
   Prepress technician: Margaret Amy Salter
Print coordinator: Katherine Berti

Text © Franklin Watts 2010
Illustration © Stefania Colnaghi 2010

First published in 2010
by Franklin Watts
(A division of Hachette
Children's Books)

Library and Archives Canada
Cataloguing in Publication

James, Robert
     How the camel got his hump / retold by Robert
James ; illustrated by Stefania Colnaghi.

(Tadpoles: tales)
"Originally written by ... Rudyard Kipling".
Issued also in electronic format.
ISBN 978-0-7787-7888-2 (bound).
--ISBN 978-0-7787-7900-1 (pbk.)

     1. Camels--Juvenile fiction. I. Kipling, Rudyard,
1865-1936 II. Colnaghi, Stefania III. Title.
IV. Series: Tadpoles (St. Catharines, Ont.). Tales

PZ7.J366Ho 2012   j823'.92
C2012-902475-9

Library of Congress
Cataloging-in-Publication Data

James, Robert.
 How the camel got his hump / retold by Robert
James ; illustrated by Gabriele Antonini.
     p. cm. -- (Tadpoles: tales)
ISBN 978-0-7787-7888-2 (reinforced library bind-
ing : alk. paper) -- ISBN 978-0-7787-7900-1 (pbk. :
alk. paper) -- ISBN 978-1-4271-7926-5 (electronic
pdf : alk. paper) -- ISBN 978-1-4271-8041-4 (elec-
tronic html : alk. paper)
     [1. Camels--Fiction.] I. Antonini, Gabriele, ill. II.
Kipling, Rudyard, 1865-1936. How the camel got
his hump. III. Title.
  PZ7.J15434Hou 2012
  [E]--dc23
                                                         2012015307

This story tries to explain
some of the different things
we see in the world today.
It was originally written by
an author called Rudyard
Kipling, over 100 years ago.

Long ago, when the world was new, there was much work to do.

The animals worked hard, but Camel was lazy.

The desert god
saw this.

"Why are you so lazy, Camel?" he asked.

"You are very rude," said the desert god.

"Humph!" said Camel.

Furious, the desert god
cast a spell.

Camel's back puffed up.

"Now you will work!"
said the desert god.

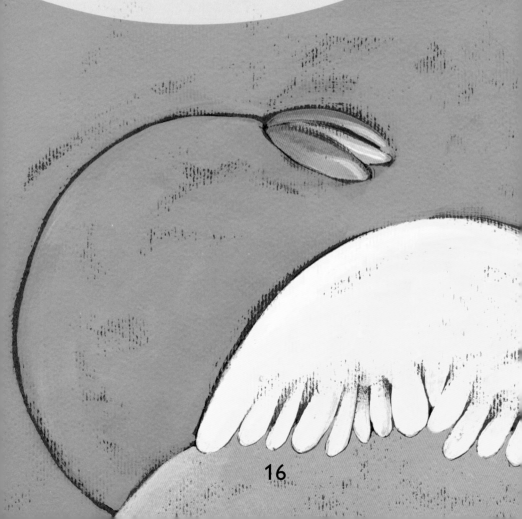

"How can I work with this on my back?" cried Camel.

17

"With that on your back, you can work for days without eating or drinking!" said the desert god.

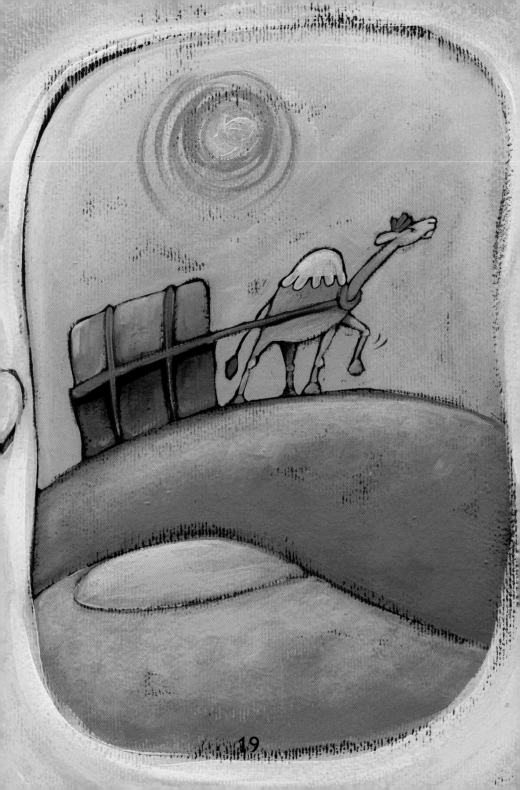

19

And that is how Camel got his humph—or hump, as we call it today.

21

Puzzle Time!

 **a**

 **b**

 **c**

 **d**

 **e**

 **f**

Put these pictures in the right order and tell the story!

rude

annoyed

lazy

angry

Which words describe Camel and which describe the desert god?

Turn the page for the answers!

Notes for adults

TADPOLES: TALES are structured for emergent readers. The books may also be used for read-alouds or shared reading with young children.

How the Camel got his Hump is based on a classic story by Rudyard Kipling. This kind of story is known as a "just-so" or "porquoi" story because it explains how something came to be. For example, many of Kipling's stories explain how certain animals developed their unique characteristics. Since young children are often curious and filled with questions, "just-so" stories make ideal reading material.

IF YOU ARE READING THIS BOOK WITH A CHILD, HERE ARE A FEW SUGGESTIONS:

1. Make reading fun! Choose a time to read when you and the child are relaxed and have time to share the story.

2. Explain that the story is called a "just so" or "pourquoi" story. *Porquoi* is a French word that means "why." Pourquoi stories are tales that explain why or how something is in the world. This information will help set a purpose for reading.

3. Encourage the child to reread the story and to retell it using his or her own words. Invite the child to use the illustrations as a guide.

4. Encourage the child to use his or her imagination to think of other "just-so" story topics. What "why" or "how" questions about animals can they think of?

5. Give praise! Children learn best in a positive environment.

HERE ARE OTHER TITLES FROM TADPOLES: TALES FOR YOU TO ENJOY:

How the Elephant got its Trunk	978-0-7787-7891-2 RLB	978-0-7787-7903-2 PB
The Ant and the Grasshopper	978-0-7787-7889-9 RLB	978-0-7787-7901-8 PB
The Boy who cried Wolf	978-0-7787-7890-5 RLB	978-0-7787-7902-5 PB
The Fox and the Crow	978-0-7787-7892-9 RLB	978-0-7787-7904-9 PB
The Lion and the Mouse	978-0-7787-7893-6 RLB	978-0-7787-7905-6 PB

VISIT WWW.CRABTREEBOOKS.COM FOR OTHER CRABTREE BOOKS.

Answers

Here is the correct order:
1. d 2. e 3. a 4. b 5. f 6. c

Words to describe Camel:
lazy, rude

Words to describe the desert god:
annoyed, angry